EDGE BOOKS

The Unexplained

NOSTRADAMUS

by **Matt Doeden**

Consultant:
Victor Baines, Founder
The Nostradamus Society of America
Fort Worth, Texas

Capstone
press®
Mankato, Minnesota

Edge Books are published by Capstone Press,
151 Good Counsel Drive, P.O. Box 669, Mankato, Minnesota 56002.
www.capstonepress.com

Library of Congress Cataloging-in-Publication Data
Doeden, Matt.
    Nostradamus / by Matt Doeden.
    p. cm.—(Edge books. The unexplained)
    Summary: "Describes the life of Nostradamus, his predictions, and
the controversy surrounding them"—Provided by publisher.
    Includes bibliographical references and index.
    ISBN–13: 978-0-7368-6760-3 (hardcover)
    ISBN–10: 0-7368-6760-0 (hardcover)
    1. Nostradamus, 1503–1566. I. Title. II. Series.
BF1815.N8D64 2006
133.3092—dc22 [B]   2006023802

Editorial Credits
Aaron Sautter, editor; Juliette Peters, set designer; Patrick D. Dentinger,
    book designer; Deirdre Barton, photo researcher/photo editor

Photo Credits
Corbis/Bettmann, 13, 14, 17; Denis Scott, 12; Fonlupt Gilles, 26, 29;
    Original Image Courtesy of NASA, 27; Reuters/Sean Adair, 23
Fortean Picture Library, 8, 19, 21, 22
Mary Evans Picture Library, cover, 5, 7, 11, 15, 18, 25

1 2 3 4 5 6 12 11 10 09 08 07

TABLE OF CONTENTS

FEATURES

Chapter 1

A Tragic Event

On a warm summer day in 1559, France's King Henry II held up a lance and charged his horse across an open field. He was jousting in a tournament against a young Scottish captain named Montgomery. But neither man could knock the other off his horse. Montgomery wanted to call the match a tie. But the king didn't agree. He insisted they continue the contest.

Learn about:
• King Henry II's death
• A famous prediction
• The Nostradamus controversy

4

Jousting was a dangerous sport.
The first man to knock his opponent
off his horse won the match.

On the next pass, Montgomery's lance struck King Henry's armor. The long wooden weapon shattered. A large splinter shot up through the king's golden visor. It plunged through his eye and into his brain. A second sharp splinter sliced into his throat. Ten days later, the king died a painful death from his wounds.

The French people were shocked by the news. But one man, Michel de Nostredame, may have foreseen the tragedy. The man, later called Nostradamus, had written a book that he claimed contained visions of the future. One of his verses, called a quatrain, read:

The young lion will overcome the older one
On a field of combat in single battle
He will pierce his eyes through a golden cage
Two wounds made one, then he dies a cruel death

Had Nostradamus foreseen King Henry's death? Many believed it. For them, Nostradamus' legend had just begun.

King Henry II ruled France from 1547 until his tragic death in 1559.

After King Henry's death, many people began
asking Nostradamus about the future.

The Greatest Seer?

Who was Nostradamus? Could he really see the future? The debate has raged for hundreds of years. His supporters call Nostradamus the greatest seer the world has ever known. They believe he really saw glimpses of the future.

Meanwhile, critics of Nostradamus say his apparent predictions are simply a matter of luck. They say it's easy to find meaning in his quatrains since his words are unclear and hard to translate. But Nostradamus' predictions still fascinate those who want a glimpse into the future.

EDGE FACT

Nostradamus wrote several almanacs containing many of his predictions. Combined with his book *The Centuries*, Nostradamus made more than 7,000 predictions about the future.

Chapter 2

EARLY LIFE LESSONS

Michel de Nostredame was born December 14, 1503, in southern France. Little is known about Nostradamus' childhood. His father sold grain, but both of his grandfathers were doctors. He studied with both of them as a child. He probably learned much about math, history, ancient languages, and astrology. By age 14 or 15, he entered the University of Avignon. Later, he studied at the University of Montpellier.

Learn about:
• Nostradamus' education
• The Bubonic plague
• A ruined reputation

In the 1500s, university classes were held in large, round rooms where all the students could see the teacher.

Nostradamus the Healer

Much of Nostradamus' studies focused on healing people. But he was also interested in other subjects. Astrology was one of his favorites. Astrology is the belief that the position of the stars and planets can affect people's lives. He also studied mysticism, which includes the use of rituals and a belief in supernatural powers.

By 1525, Nostradamus earned his medical license. Around the same time, the bubonic plague hit France. The plague was a terrible disease that killed many people as it spread from town to town. Nostradamus quickly made a name for himself as a healer. He had new ideas on how to treat sick people. He gave his patients special herbs and fresh water. He also told them to go outside and breathe in the fresh air.

In astrology, each ➤ month of the year is given a sign.

Nostradamus' reputation as a healer grew. People all over Europe sent for his help. During this time, Nostradamus kept practicing astrology. His reputation in this area grew as well. Soon, he was also writing horoscopes and giving readings to people.

Nostradamus studied the stars and planets to write horoscopes for people.

Personal Tragedy

Nostradamus soon married and started a family. Life was good. But everything changed in 1537. Nostradamus' family became sick with the plague, and he was unable to save them. The death of his family was a crushing blow.

Things soon got even worse. During the 1500s, people's religious beliefs were controlled by the Inquisition. The Inquisition often falsely accused and punished people for crimes against the Catholic Church. One day Nostradamus saw men putting up a statue of Mary, the mother of Jesus. He made a joke about them "casting demons." The Inquisition tried to arrest Nostradamus for the crime of heresy. At age 33, Nostradamus' future looked very bleak.

The Inquisition accused and punished many people for crimes they didn't commit.

The Bubonic Plague

The bubonic plague was one of the deadliest diseases in human history. The disease was carried and spread by fleas that lived in the fur of rats and other rodents. Human victims of the plague suffered from chills and fever. They also had painful swelling in their necks and armpits as the disease built up in their blood.

During Nostradamus' time, doctors often treated sick people by cutting them and letting their blood flow out. They believed the blood carried the sickness out of the body. But "bleeding" the patients only made things worse. It made patients too weak to fight the disease naturally. Thousands of people died from the plague.

Chapter 3

NOSTRADAMUS THE SEER

Before his trial for heresy could begin, Nostradamus left France. He escaped to Italy, where he lived for about seven years. During this time, he kept studying astrology. But when the plague again struck France, he returned to help.

Visions of the Future

Nostradamus moved to the French town of Salon. By helping plague victims, he soon regained some respect as a healer. In 1547, he remarried and started a new family. He also continued his study of mysticism. Before long, he began claiming to have visions of the future.

Learn about:
- Seeing visions
- A new career
- Predicting 9/11

Nostradamus spent many hours
each day studying astrology and
other forms of mysticism.

To see his visions, Nostradamus sat on a type of stool with three legs, called a tripod. A steaming bowl of water with herbs and oils sat under him. He then gazed into a bowl of water while a single candle burned before him. Nostradamus believed God sent him visions of the future in the bowl of water.

▲ Nostradamus often gave advice to France's Queen Catherine.

The Centuries

In 1554, Nostradamus published the first volume of his most famous book, *The Centuries*. The book was popular among rich, educated people. Some even asked for his advice. But many in the Catholic Church were afraid of Nostradamus' strange and scary predictions. Some people even thought Nostradamus worked for the devil.

Nostradamus' book is also called *The Prophecies*. ➤

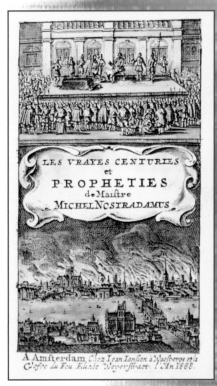

One of Nostradamus' biggest supporters was the French queen, Catherine. Nostradamus often did horoscope readings for Catherine's husband, King Henry II, and her children. One day, he warned her about the king's possible death in combat. Catherine believed Nostradamus' warning, but the king wouldn't listen. Henry's death in 1559 sealed Nostradamus' place as France's most famous seer.

Queen Catherine enjoyed reading the horoscopes Nostradamus wrote for her family.

Nostradamus was buried in the wall of a church in Salon, France. A statue honors his memory.

For the next seven years, Nostradamus continued to make and publish predictions. But in 1566, he became sick. On the morning of July 2, he was found dead beside his bed. His secretary later shared the conversation they'd had the night before. Nostradamus had said to him, "You will not find me alive by sunrise." If the story is true, it was Nostradamus' final prediction.

A Prediction for 9/11?

After the terrorist attacks of September 11, 2001, rumors swirled that Nostradamus had predicted the event. Many Internet sites quoted a quatrain that seemed to foretell the violent attacks. But the quatrain was a hoax. Someone had pieced together lines from other quatrains to make it seem like a real prediction. Still, Nostradamus supporters say a few quatrains do refer to the tragic events.

Chapter 4

LOOKING FOR ANSWERS

Those who believe in Nostradamus' powers point to many events that he may have foreseen. His supporters say he predicted the rise of Adolf Hitler and the death of President John F. Kennedy. They also say he foresaw the invention of the radio, lightbulb, and atomic bomb. Some claim that he predicted the American and French Revolutions, World Wars I and II, and even the first moon landing.

Were these predictions real? Or are they the result of people's imaginations and poor translation? Some believe Nostradamus really saw these events. They say his quatrains are filled with real predictions, secret codes, and more. Others believe there's nothing special about his verses.

Learn about:
- Nostradamus' critics
- Translation problems
- Famous predictions

Adolf Hitler was a German dictator who started World War II. Some people believe Nostradamus predicted his rise to power.

Lost in Translation

Various translations are often a major problem with Nostradamus' predictions. His original works were written by hand more than 400 years ago. Translating his writing from the original French to modern English can be difficult.

One example of different translations comes from a quatrain some people think calls the United States by name. One translation ends, "The victor born on American soil." But other translations of the same line read differently. One reads, "The youngest shall be the conqueror of Armorick country." Still another reads, "Victor the younger in the land of Brittany." All these different versions show the impact each translation can have on even a single line.

▲ **Nostradamus' original writings are hard to read and translate.**

Famous Predictions

Nostradamus' supporters credit him with many predictions. Some of his most famous predictions are listed here.

- The death of King Henry II
- The assassination of President John F. Kennedy
- The rise of Napoleon and the French Revolution
- The American Revolution
- World Wars I and II
- The stock market crash of 1929
- The rise of Adolf Hitler
- Creation and use of the atomic bomb
- The first moon landing
- The explosion of the space shuttle *Challenger*
- His own death

Despite the critics, believers still claim Nostradamus really saw the future. They say his quatrains hint at too many real events to simply be lucky guesses. But one thing is certain. Nostradamus is the most famous seer in history. Dozens of books have been written about him. Several movies and TV shows center on his life and works. He's been dead for more than 400 years, but he continues to fascinate us today.

Was Nostradamus a true seer? Did his visions come from God? We can't really know for sure. All we can do is look at the evidence and decide for ourselves.

Nostradamus' life and works continue to fascinate people. Will all of his predictions come true one day?

GLOSSARY

astrology (uh-STROL-uh-jee)—the study of how the positions of the stars and planets affect people's lives

dictator (DIK-tay-tur)—someone who has complete control of a country, often ruling it unjustly

heresy (HER-uh-see)—actions or opinions that are different from those of a particular religion and unacceptable to people in authority

horoscope (HOR-uh-skope)—a reading of the position of the stars and planets and how they might affect a person's life

Inquisition (in-kwa-ZI-shun)—a former court of the Catholic Church that often accused and cruelly punished people for heresy from the late 1400s to the early 1800s

mysticism (MIS-tuh-si-zem)—the belief that supernatural knowledge can be obtained through a spiritual experience

plague (PLAYG)—a deadly disease that spreads quickly; waves of bubonic plague swept through Europe between the 1300s and 1500s.

quatrain (KWA-trayn)—the name for the four-lined verses in which Nostradamus wrote most of his predictions

READ MORE

Kallen, Stuart A. *Fortune-Telling*. The Mystery Library. San Diego: Lucent Books, 2004.

Martin, Michael. *ESP: Extrasensory Perception*. The Unexplained. Mankato, Minn.: Capstone Press, 2006.

Roleff, Tamara L., ed. *Psychics*. Fact or Fiction? San Diego: Greenhaven Press, 2003.

INTERNET SITES

FactHound offers a safe, fun way to find Internet sites related to this book. All of the sites on FactHound have been researched by our staff.

Here's how:
1. Visit *www.facthound.com*
2. Choose your grade level.
3. Type in this book ID code **0736867600** for age-appropriate sites. You may also browse subjects by clicking on letters, or by clicking on pictures and words.
4. Click on the **Fetch It** button.

FactHound will fetch the best sites for you!

INDEX